KLASKY
CSUPO INC.

Based on the TV series *Rugrats*® created by Arlene Klasky, Gabor Csupo,
and Paul Germain as seen on Nickelodeon®

SIMON SPOTLIGHT
An imprint of Simon & Schuster Children's Publishing Division
1230 Avenue of the Americas, New York, New York 10020

Manufactured in the United States of America

First Edition   10 9 8 7 6 5 4 3 2 1

ISBN 0-689-82538-2

more jokes!

by David Lewman

Simon Spotlight/Nickelodeon

What do dinosaurs put on their fish sandwiches?
Reptartar sauce.

Knock, knock.
Who's there?
Turnip.
Turnip who?
Turn up the lights—I'm scared!

Knock, knock.
Who's there?
Candy.
Candy who?
Can Didi give us a treat?

Was the potty surprised when Chuckie first used it?
Yes, it was a little throne.

What did Stu get when he tried to grill cabbage?
Coal slaw.

How is Spike standing on wet grass like a late library book?
They're both over dew.

What do pigs use to write top-secret messages?
Invisible oink.

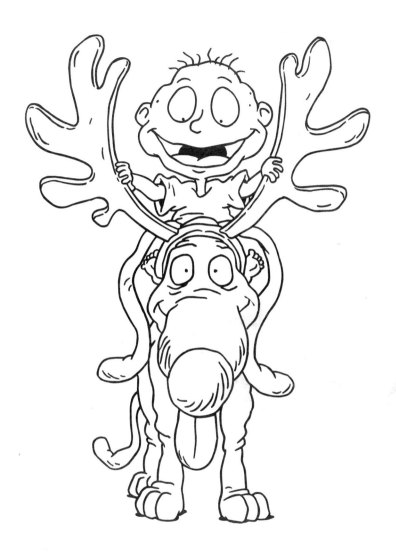

Why did Angelica try to drive the female deer nuts?
She wanted to see a kooky doe.

Chuckie: Angelica, why did you pour that sack of powder onto the grass?
Angelica: Because, you dumb baby, I wanted to make a flour garden!

Who likes yucky stuff better: Phil or the son of the supermarket owner?
The son, because he's a little grocer.

What do you get when you cross a pig with a wildcat?
Sausage lynx.

What game does Dil play on top of a mountain?
Peakaboo.

What has smooth skin, a fluffy
bun, and flies?
A plane hot dog.

Why does Angelica carry a
pair of those little golf spikes?
Because she loves two tees.

How did the Reptar wagon feel after it got new wheels?
Tired.

What did the lost calf say to the baby?
"I want my mooommy!"

Why didn't Tommy answer the phone?
The phone had crawl-waiting.

Tommy: What do you like to hear before you go to sleep?
Phil: A Lil-a-bye!

What's the difference between a baby and a duck with no taste?
One's a wacky toddler and the other's a tacky waddler.

Tommy: If you two were cats, what kind would you be?
Phil and Lil: Copycats!

If Chuckie were a cat, what kind would he be?
A scaredy-cat.

What is the babies' favorite dinosaur called when he's late?
Reptardy.

Why did the sheep take dance lessons?
She wanted to be a baaaaaallerina.

Knock, knock.
Who's there?
Shh.
Shh who?
Hey, I'm not a fly!

**If Tommy's cousin were an antelope,
what would she be?**
A gazellica.

What do cats use to cut the grass?
A lawnmeower.

Lil: Why did Angelica push everyone off the dance floor?

Susie: She wanted to be a bully dancer.

What do you call Tommy's cousin after she falls in the garbage?
Ansmellyca.

Which tool makes the Pickleses' car go?
A Stu-driver.

**Why does Grandpa Lou call his teeth
"Niagara"?**
Because they're falls.

Knock, knock.
Who's there?
Snakie.
Snakie who?
'S nakie Tommy—I kicked off my diaper!

How long has Tommy's dad been able to walk?
Ever since he could stand on his own
Stu feet.

How is spinning Angelica like unplugging a TV?
Either way, you turn a show-off.

Why did Lil get under the covers?
She wanted to fill in the blankie.

Why did Lil hop over to Tommy's grandpa?
She wanted to skip to the Lou.

**If Phil and Lil's dad were in
"The Wizard of Oz," who
would he play?**
The Howardly Lion.

**What does a sheep
use to carry its books?**
A baaaaaackpack.

Chuckie: Tommy, why did you roll a bunch of logs into your bedroom?
Tommy: I wanted to have a lumber party!

What does the babies' favorite dinosaur call himself when he's in Hollywood?
Repstar.

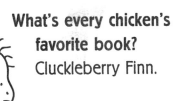

What's every chicken's
favorite book?
Cluckleberry Finn.

Why did Tommy
crawl on the hood of
his dad's car?
He heard that it
needed a new
windshield diaper.

How did the lion make all his money?
As a roar-to-roar salesman.

Why did the duck keep doing somersaults?
He wanted to be a quackrobat.

What did the snake say to his girlfriend?
"C'mon, let's hiss and make up."

What's every sheep's favorite sport?
Baaaaadminton.

When is Dil like the kid in "Free Willy"?
When he lets out a wail.

**If Didi's father were a dinosaur, what kind
would he be?**
A tyranno-Boris rex.

What does Charlotte say when asking Angelica to choose between a tricycle and a Reptar bar?
"Trike or treat?"

Why do birds sing when they're hungry?
They get the urge tweet.

Who can help Chuckie
get over his fear of riding
a tricycle?
A trike-ologist.

Lil: Why did you invite a
hog to eat outdoors?
Phil: I wanted to have a pignic!

Knock, knock.
Who's there?
Street.
Street who?
'S treat time, isn't it?

Who would Tommy's cousin be if she'd been raised by apes?
Tarzangelica.

What did the belly button say just before it left?
"I'm outtie here!"

Was the baby bird like his dad?
Yes, he was a chirp off the old block.

What do you get when you cross a bunny and a puppy?
A hop dog.

Who's every sheep's favorite superhero?
Baaaaatman.

How does Chuckie like his hamburger?
Medium scared.

What did Abe Lincoln drink when he was a baby?
The bottle of Gettysburg.

What do Phil and Lil do before playing any sport?
They worm up.

What's funny about Chuckie's glasses?
He needs SQUARES to look aROUND!

Angelica: Why are you afraid of kings and queens?

Chuckie: I heard they wear clowns on their heads.

What did Chuckie's left cheek say to his right cheek?

"Look out, we've been spotted!"

What do you get when you cross an anteater and a dog?
An aardbark.

What kind of stories does Grandpa Lou tell in the car?
Toll tales.

Phil: Why did you climb on Spike's back in the yard?
Tommy: I like to sit out on the pooch.

How is Spike like a telephone?
He has collar I. D.

What do you call five babies fighting over Halloween treats?
Candy-monium.

How is Chuckie's nose like a teddy bear?

They're both stuffed.

What's cold, tasty, and great for fixing your hair?
An ice-cream comb!

What do cats like to eat on hot days?
Mice-cream cones.

What did Phil say to Lil when she stole his snack?
"You took the worms right out of my mouth, Lillian."

Why did the police interrupt Tommy's afternoon snooze?
They heard there'd been a kid napping.

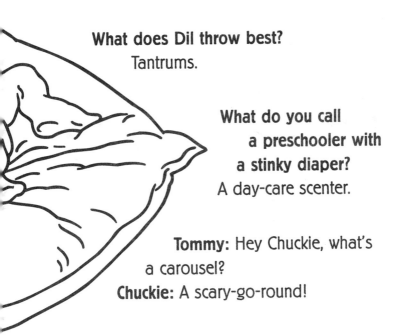

Why did Dil grab the cloth around Tommy's neck?
Bibling rivalry.

What does Dil throw best?
Tantrums.

What do you call a preschooler with a stinky diaper?
A day-care scenter.

Tommy: Hey Chuckie, what's a carousel?
Chuckie: A scary-go-round!

Why did Spike go to school?
He wanted to be the
teacher's pet.

What do you call Reptar after he falls down the stairs?
A dinosore.

Phil: What did you say to the chicken who didn't make the barnyard choir?
Lil: Better cluck next time!

Why did Phil paint squares on his suitcase?
He wanted to check his baggage.

How is Angelica like a new doctor?
They both need more patience.

What do the babies call their favorite dinosaur with a sore throat?
Streptar.

What do you call newborn babies like
Phil and Lil?
Twinfants!

Why did Dil put a "B" on his knee?
He wanted to be a B-knee baby.

Knock, knock.
Who's there?
Pizza.
Pizza who?
Pete's a friend of mine . . . is he here?

What do diapered babies like to play?
Follow-the-leaker.

What does Chuckie's father cook on the grill?
Chasburgers.

If Tommy's brother were a flower, what kind would he be?
A daffo-Dil.

What do you get when you cross Tommy's cousin with an ape?
An orangutangelica.

Susie: Was Dr. Lipschitz's clinic a bargain for your family?
Tommy: Yes, we got a really good Dil!